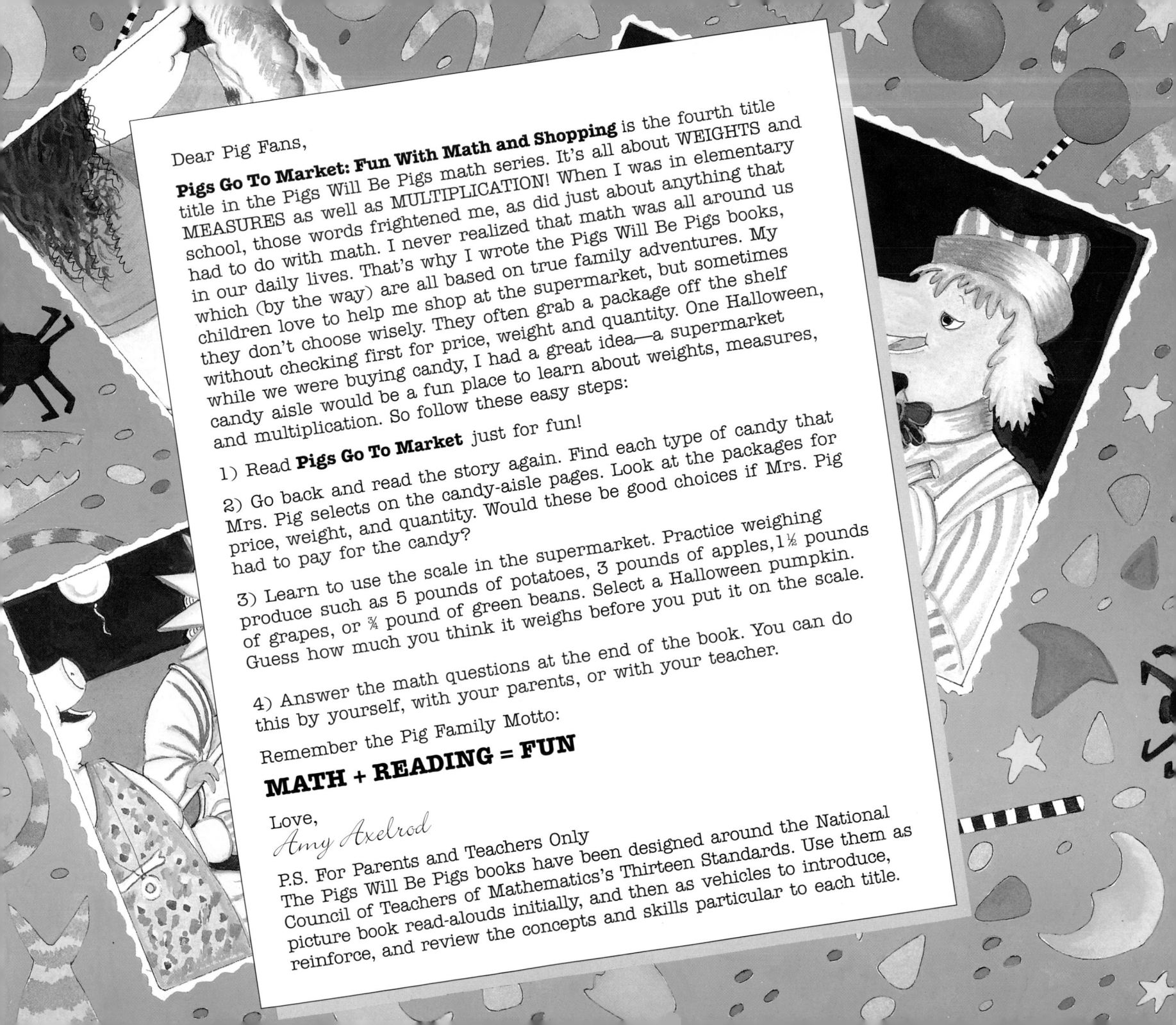

Dear Pig Fans,

Pigs Go To Market: Fun With Math and Shopping is the fourth title in the Pigs Will Be Pigs math series. It's all about WEIGHTS and MEASURES as well as MULTIPLICATION! When I was in elementary school, those words frightened me, as did just about anything that had to do with math. I never realized that math was all around us in our daily lives. That's why I wrote the Pigs Will Be Pigs books, which (by the way) are all based on true family adventures. My children love to help me shop at the supermarket, but sometimes they don't choose wisely. They often grab a package off the shelf without checking first for price, weight and quantity. One Halloween, while we were buying candy, I had a great idea—a supermarket candy aisle would be a fun place to learn about weights, measures, and multiplication. So follow these easy steps:

1) Read **Pigs Go To Market** just for fun!

2) Go back and read the story again. Find each type of candy that Mrs. Pig selects on the candy-aisle pages. Look at the packages for price, weight, and quantity. Would these be good choices if Mrs. Pig had to pay for the candy?

3) Learn to use the scale in the supermarket. Practice weighing produce such as 5 pounds of potatoes, 3 pounds of apples, 1½ pounds of grapes, or ¾ pound of green beans. Select a Halloween pumpkin. Guess how much you think it weighs before you put it on the scale.

4) Answer the math questions at the end of the book. You can do this by yourself, with your parents, or with your teacher.

Remember the Pig Family Motto:

MATH + READING = FUN

Love,

Amy Axelrod

P.S. For Parents and Teachers Only
The Pigs Will Be Pigs books have been designed around the National Council of Teachers of Mathematics's Thirteen Standards. Use them as picture book read-alouds initially, and then as vehicles to introduce, reinforce, and review the concepts and skills particular to each title.

Pigs go to Market

Fun with Math and Shopping

story by **Amy Axelrod**

pictures by **Sharon McGinley-Nally**

Aladdin Paperbacks

The Pigs were in a pickle.

"I can't believe my eyes!" exclaimed Mrs. Pig. "There's not a piece of Halloween candy left in this house. We've got a dozen guests coming in one hour."

"We're sorry," said Grandma Pig. "I guess we got carried away."

"You can say that again," said Mrs. Pig. "Only now what are we supposed to do?"

"No problem," said Mr. Pig. "It won't be dark for quite a while. We've got plenty of time to run out to the supermarket before our party guests start arriving."

"Great idea," said Mrs. Pig, "except for one thing."

"What's that?" asked Mr. Pig.

"Do you really think we're dressed for shopping?" she asked.

"Oh, c'mon Mom," said the piglets.

"Go on ahead," said Grandma and Grandpa Pig. "We'll take care of everything on the home front."

"Well then, family," said Mr. Pig.

LET'S

HIT THE ROAD!

The parking lot was packed.
"Look how crowded it is," said Mr. Pig. "You'd think they were giving food away."
"That'll be the day," laughed Mrs. Pig.
The Pigs parked the car and made their way to the entrance of the supermarket.

"CONGRATULATIONS!" proclaimed the store manager to Mrs. Pig as the door swung open. "You're our one millionth customer!"

"Me?" asked Mrs. Pig.

"That's right," he said. "And have we got a Halloween treat for you! How does a five-minute shopping spree sound?"

"How much can I spend?" asked Mrs. Pig.

"Sky's the limit," answered the store manager.

Mrs. Pig took off.
 "Dear, I'm so proud of you!"
called Mr. Pig.

Mrs. Pig skipped aisle one
but braked at aisle two for
canned goods. She cleaned
out the entire top and bottom
rows of soups and sauces.

"We'll meet you in the candy
aisle, Mom!" yelled the piglets.

Mrs. Pig whipped around the corner and trotted over to aisle four to the display of Halloween candy. She quickly chose six packs of Ghouly Drops and three bags of Jelly Spiders. Then Mrs. Pig went for four buckets of Pound O' Pumpkins, which were next to the Wiggly Worms on the shelf.

"Mrs. Pig, you have three minutes left," warned a voice on the loudspeaker.

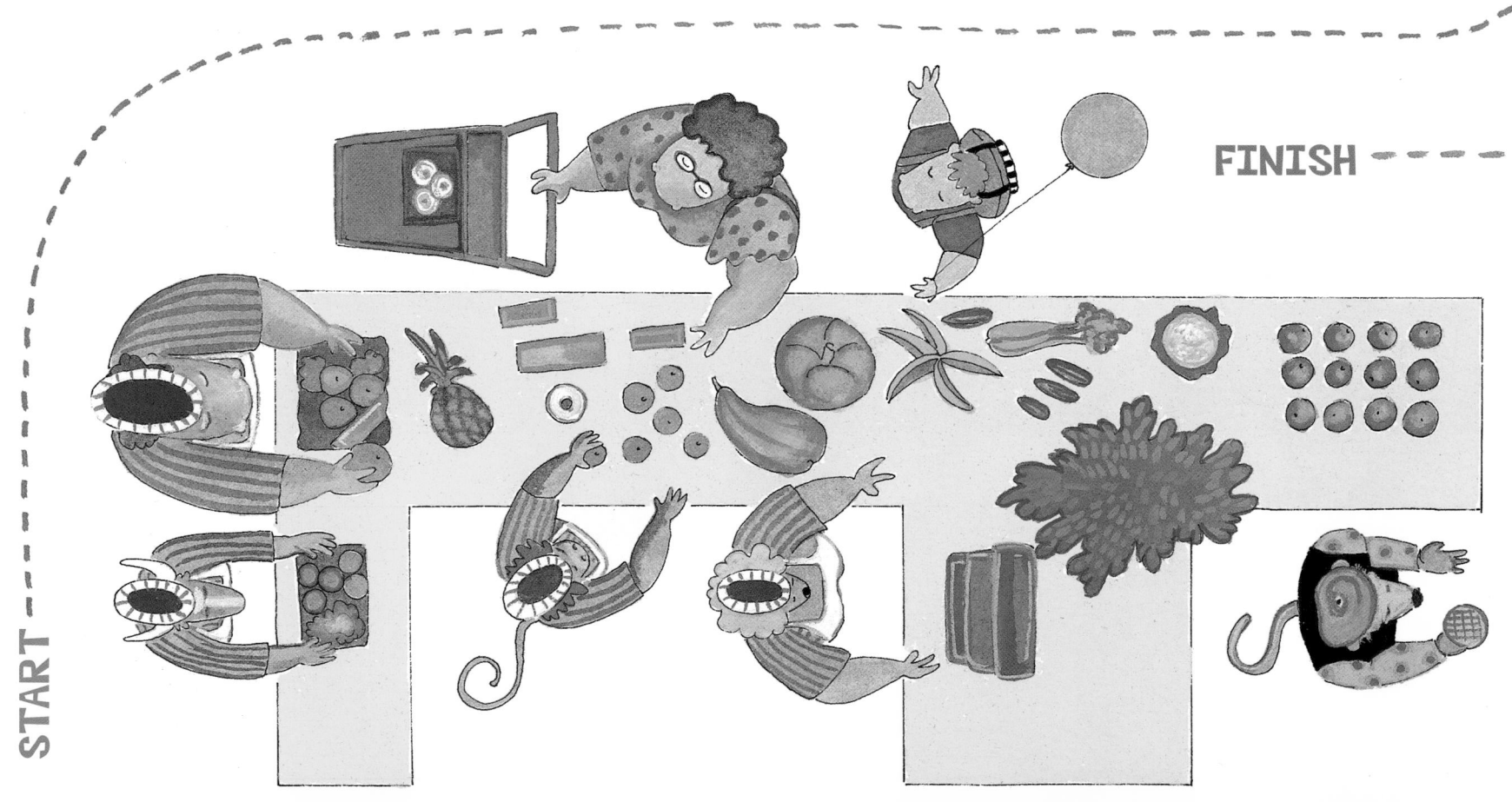

START

FINISH

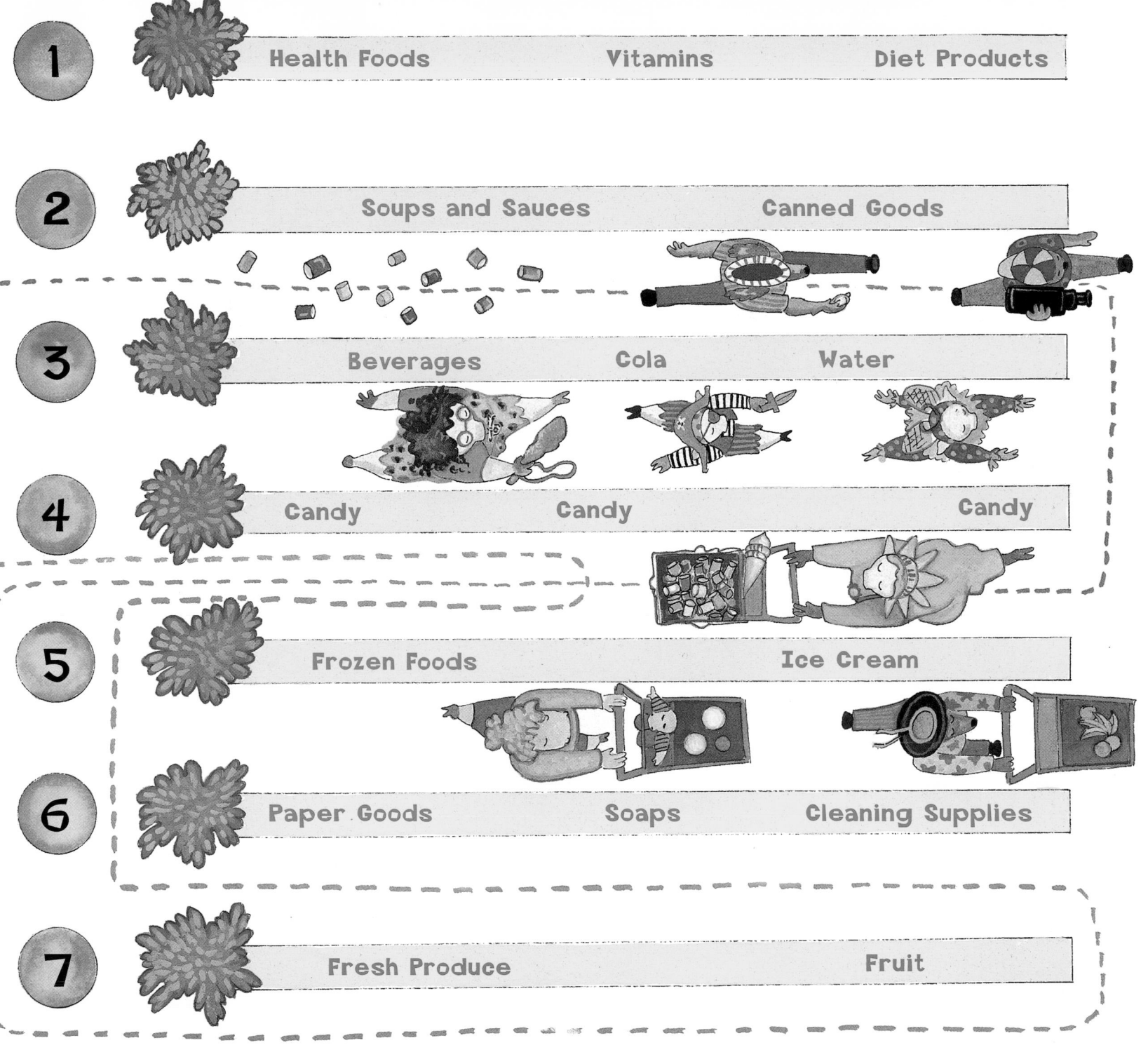

"Ooh, Witches Brooms!"
Mrs. Pig said excitedly as she grabbed two medium-sized boxes from
the shelf above. "Children," she asked the piglets, "want to try some?"
The piglets shook their heads no.
"What's that in your mouths?" asked Mrs. Pig.

The piglets mumbled something.

"Red Hot Jumbos!" exclaimed Mrs. Pig as she pried their mouths open. "How many do you have stuffed in there? You know they're bad for your teeth."

"Oh, sweetie," said Mr. Pig. "One box won't hurt. I think you'd better hurry up now, the clock is ticking."

"Mrs. Pig, you have two minutes left."

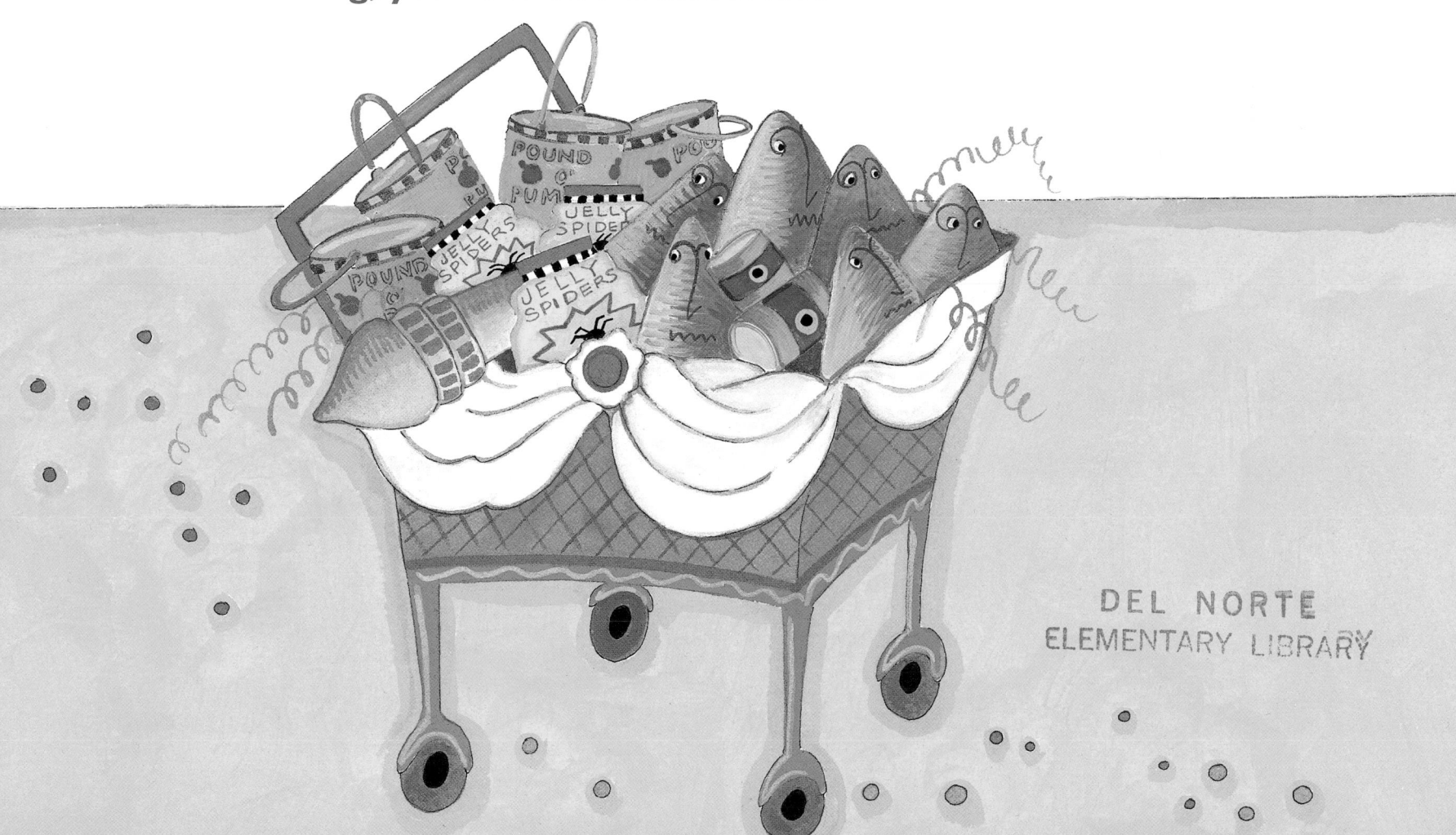

"I'm off," said Mrs. Pig and she rolled toward aisle seven for fresh produce. She loaded the wagon with broccoli and cantaloupes, and then she picked a perfect pair of matching pumpkins for the piglets.

Mrs. Pig waved to the crowd and blew kisses
to Mr. Pig as she sailed by and headed down
aisle six for some paper goods and cleaning
supplies.

"Mrs. Pig, you have one minute left."

"Go, Mom, go!"

"Dear!" called Mr. Pig. "I think you forgot the
Wiggly Worms. It won't be a party without them."

Mrs. Pig broke into a sweat as she zipped around
the corner and zoomed back to aisle four.

"Mrs. Pig, you have ten seconds left."

Mrs. Pig grabbed one economy-sized jar of Wiggly Worms
and raced to the checkout line in the nick of time. It took
four clerks to pack up Mrs. Pig's haul into twelve shopping bags.

"Look at the sky," said Mrs. Pig as they walked out to the parking lot. "We'd better hurry home."

"Well, that shopping adventure was certainly an unexpected treat," said Mr. Pig.

"I'm exhausted," said Mrs. Pig.

"We're hungry," said the piglets.

"I hope Grandma and Grandpa didn't have any trouble," said Mrs. Pig.

"Dear, what we need is a little pick-me-up." said Mr. Pig. "Are you thinking what I'm thinking?"

Mrs. Pig broke open the candy while Mr. Pig drove home.

"Wow!" said the piglets.

"Take a look at that crowd!" said Mr. Pig. "Was our guest list that large?"

"Dear, pass the candy in a hurry. I can't believe my . . .

THE PIGS ATE ALL OF THE HALLOWEEN CANDY ON THE RIDE HOME!

They ate GHOULY DROPS

Pack 1
Five rows of four gumdrops
5 X 4

+

Pack 2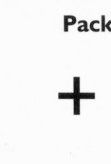
Five rows of four gumdrops
5 X 4

+

Pack 3
Five rows of four gumdrops
5 X 4

+

Pack 4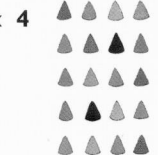
Five rows of four gumdrops
5 X 4

+

Pack 5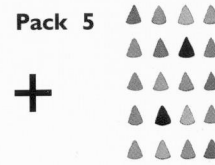
Five rows of four gumdrops
5 X 4

+

Pack 6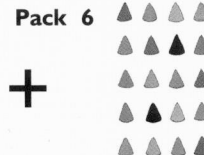
Five rows of four gumdrops
5 X 4

PLUS JELLY SPIDERS

Bag 1
Three rows of eight spiders
3 X 8

+

Bag 2
Three rows of eight spiders
3 X 8

+

Bag 3
Three rows of eight spiders
3 X 8

PLUS POUND O' PUMPKINS

Bucket 1
Four rows of four pumpkins
4 X 4

+

Bucket 2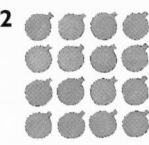
Four rows of four pumpkins
4 X 4

+

Bucket 3
Four rows of four pumpkins
4 X 4

+

Bucket 4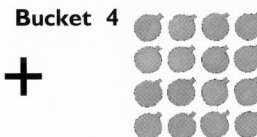
Four rows of four pumpkins
4 X 4

PLUS WITCHES BROOMS

Box 1
Four rows of nine brooms
4 X 9

+

Box 2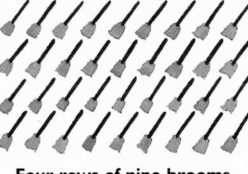
Four rows of nine brooms
4 X 9

PLUS RED HOT JUMBOS

Box 1
Three rows of four jumbos
3 X 4

PLUS WIGGLY WORMS

Jar 1
Eight rows of ten worms
8 X 10

MEASUREMENT FACTS

16 ounces = 1 pound

2,000 pounds = 1 ton

When you want to know what an object weighs you use a unit of measure called the pound. Each pound is made up of 16 ounces. An ounce is 1/16 of a pound. The abbreviation for an ounce is OZ., and the abbreviation for a pound is LB. The instrument used when you weigh something is called a scale.

How many pieces of Halloween candy did the Pigs eat in all?

If the Pigs had to pay for all of the candy, how much would it have cost?

How many unexpected guests came to the party?

Bonus Question: How much did all of the candy that the Pigs ate weigh?

First Aladdin Paperbacks edition August 1999

Text copyright © 1997 by Amy Axelrod

Illustrations copyright © 1997 by Sharon McGinley-Nally

Aladdin Paperbacks

An imprint of Simon & Schuster Children's Publishing Division

1230 Avenue of the Americas

New York, NY 10020

All rights reserved including the right of reproduction in whole or in part in any form.

Also available in a Simon & Schuster Books for Young Readers hardcover edition.

Designed by Anahid Hamparian

The text of this book is set in 17-point Baskerville.

The illustrations are rendered in inks, watercolors, and acrylics.

Printed in Hong Kong

10 9 8 7 6 5 4

The Library of Congress has cataloged the hardcover edition as follows:

Axelrod, Amy.

Pigs go to market : Fun with Math and shopping / story by Amy Axelrod; pictures by Sharon McGinley-Nally. p. cm.

Summary: Concepts of price and quantity enter the picture when Mrs. Pig wins a five-minute shopping spree at the supermarket.

ISBN 0-689-81069-5

[1. Pigs–Fiction. 2. Mathematics–Fiction. 3. Shopping–Fiction.]

I. McGinley-Nally, Sharon, ill. II. Title.

PZ7.A96155Pd 1997

[E]–dc20 96-25566

ISBN 0-689-82553-6 (Aladdin pbk.)

For Virginia A. Duncan, Editor and Jelly Bean Aficionado

—A. A.

For my bright and shining friend, Harimandir

—S. M-N.

Note: I ounce (OZ.) = 28.350 grams (g)

All weights on candy packages have been rounded off.